This book belongs to:

....

....

For Mum & Dad
C.C.

To Lara Pippa, with oodles of love xx
J.McC.

Reading Consultant: Prue Goodwin, Lecturer in literacy and children's books

ORCHARD BOOKS
338 Euston Road, London NW1 3BH
Orchard Books Australia
Hachette Children's Books
Level 17/207 Kent Street, Sydney NSW 2000

First published in 2011 by Orchard Books
First paperback publication in 2012

Text © Catherine Coe 2011
Illustrations © Jan McCafferty 2011

ISBN 978 1 40830 683 3 (hardback)
ISBN 978 1 40830 691 8 (paperback)

The rights of Catherine Coe to be identified as the author and
Jan McCafferty to be identified as the illustrator of this work
have been asserted by them in accordance with the
Copyright, Designs and Patents Act, 1988.

1 3 5 7 9 10 8 6 4 2 (hardback)
1 3 5 7 9 10 8 6 4 2 (paperback)

Printed in China

Orchard Books is a division of Hachette Children's Books,
an Hachette UK company.

www.hachette.co.uk

The New
Hide-out

Written by
Catherine Coe **Illustrated by**
Jan McCafferty

ORCHARD

Casper loved being a cowboy. He rode his horse and swung his lasso until his arms ached! "Yee-ha!"

It was even more fun when his best friend, Pete, was with him. And when the two cowboys needed a rest, they went to their treehouse hide-out.

But today, Pete wasn't happy. "We need a new hide-out!" he said. "This one is much too old and much too small."

Casper looked around the hide-out. "OK!" he agreed. It would be exciting to find somewhere new.

But their hide-out had been great fun, too. Casper was a bit sad to leave it behind.

Would they find anywhere better?

"Come on, Casper," said Pete, galloping away on his horse, Funny Fool. "We'll find a great new hide-out nearby!"

Casper mounted his horse,
Blue the Brave. "OK, partner,"
he replied. "But it has to be
just *perfect*!"

Casper and his best friend galloped along, until Pete suddenly stopped. "Aha," he said. "This is just right!"

They had reached Lake Ho Ho.
Pete pointed to a cove on the
other side.
"It looks pretty good!" Casper
agreed.

The two excited cowboys rode around the lake towards their new hide-out.
They unpacked their belongings, and made themselves at home.

"Argh!" Casper suddenly yelled. He was getting wet!

He looked down and saw the lake water lapping at his blanket!

"This won't do," Pete said.

Pete and Casper packed up all their belongings and mounted their horses again.

"Don't worry," Pete told Casper. "We will find a new hide-out."

Casper wasn't so sure, but he followed Pete and hoped he was right.

Casper was just starting to get hungry when Pete stopped and pointed at a spot of grassland. "What about there?" Pete asked.

Casper agreed to give it a try.
At least they could have lunch!
He left Blue to graze, and was
about to sit down when . . .

"... Ouch!"

Casper jumped right back up
again. He had sat on a cactus!
Their new hide-out was home
to lots of very prickly plants.

"This is no good," Casper said.
"It hurts here!"
"You're right," Pete replied. "But we mustn't give up just yet!"

They rode on towards the
desert plains.

Just as Casper was getting tired,
Pete shouted, "Now *that* is the
perfect hide-out!"

Casper looked up and saw
a cave in the mountainside.
"Yes, perfect!" he said.

Casper and Pete tied up Blue and Funny Fool and sat down in their new hide-out. It had been a long day, and soon the two cowboys were fast asleep.

Casper was woken by a tickling on his neck. He opened his eyes and saw . . . a snake!

"Argh!" Casper cried. "We can't stay here!"
The two cowboys left the cave *very* quickly.

It was getting dark and they
still hadn't found a new
hide-out.

"We should go back," Casper
said sadly.

"OK, Casper," Pete agreed.

As their ranches came into sight, Casper had an idea. He could see another hide-out, right there in his back yard. "Let's go!" he said to Pete.

As soon as they went round the corner, Pete knew exactly what Casper was thinking.

At the top of a tree stood their old, cosy hide-out.

"All right!"
the cowboys
shouted
together.
They climbed the tree quickly
and unpacked their belongings.

There was no
rising water . . .

there were no
prickly cactus
plants . . .

and there were
no sneaky
snakes!

It was perfect!

Written by **Illustrated by**
Catherine Coe   **Jan McCafferty**

All priced at £8.99

Orchard Books are available from all good bookshops,
or can be ordered from our website: www.orchardbooks.co.uk,
or telephone 01235 827702, or fax 01235 827703.

Prices and availability are subject to change.